I like to be Kind

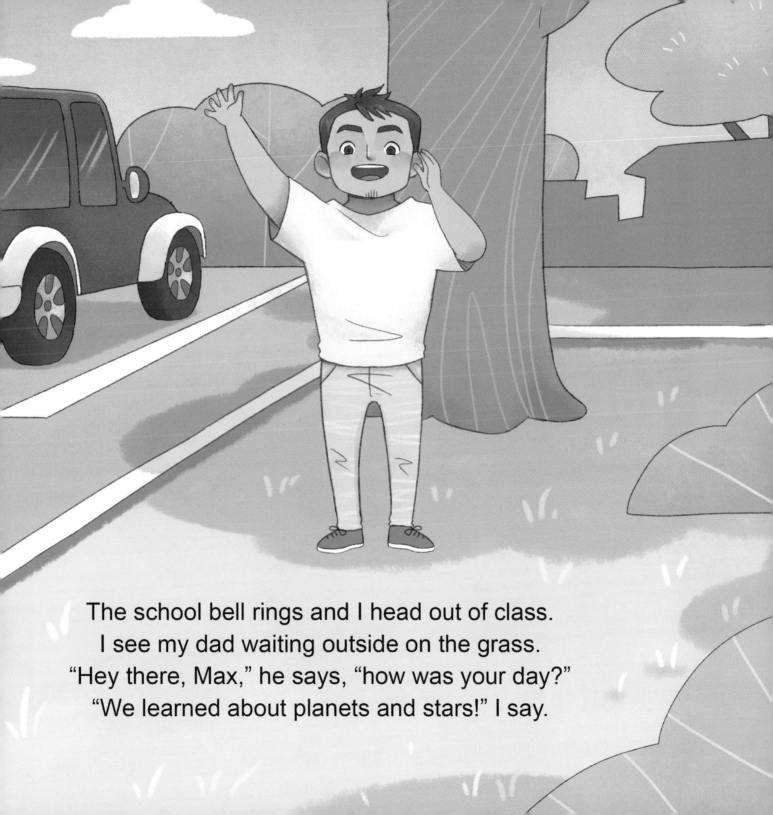

The school bell rings and I head out of class.
I see my dad waiting outside on the grass.
"Hey there, Max," he says, "how was your day?"
"We learned about planets and stars!" I say.

On our walk home, we see a small puppy.
My dad says, "Oh, no! He's limping and muddy."
We look at his collar and see his name: Brett.
My dad says, "We have to take Brett to the vet."

The poor little puppy cries all the way there.
In the vet's lobby, we fill out a questionnaire.
Just before we go home, I ask my dad why
we helped someone's dog and didn't just walk by.

He said, "Kindness matters. We should do what we can to make this world better and lend a helping hand. Brett was hurt badly. It was the right thing to do. I hope that you will always choose kindness too."

On our walk the next morning, we pass a sad man.
He's next to the curb fixing a flat tire on his van.
I catch the man's eye, wave, and smile extra wide.
He laughs and waves back. My heart fills with pride.

When we get to school, I say goodbye to my dad.
I will ask my teacher what kind of morning she's had.
I say, "Hi, Miss Olsen, are you having a nice day?"
"Yes, thank you for asking. It's been great I must say."

At recess I play soccer with my good friend, Lee.
I notice our classmate standing alone by a tree.
I run up to him and ask, "Do you want to play?"
He says, "You bet, Max. Thank you for making my day."

Later at home, I think of a new way to be kind.
Phoning my grandparents is what comes to mind.
My mom dials their number, then I hear Grandma's voice.
"Is this my sweet Max calling?" I hear her rejoice.

"Yes, Grandma, it's me. How are Grandpa and you?
I'm just calling to say I love and miss you."
I hear Grandma say, "Max, we feel just the same.
We will visit this weekend." "Yippy!" I exclaim.

It's a nice summer evening and my family and I
are out on the porch watching the clouds in the sky.
My dad says, "Max, please tell us about your day."
I say, "Lee and I asked a new friend to play."

"I remembered what you said, Dad. I chose to be kind.
It made me feel great because I kept kindness in mind.
On my walk to school, I made a man's frown go away."
I called my grandparents and brightened my teacher's day.

"I'm so proud of you, son," my mom says to me.
I stand up to hug her. Then, guess what I see?
The same little puppy, with a bandage on his knee,
being carried by his owner, as content as can be.

The End

Hi,

My name is Aleks Harrison. I am the author of children's books about emotions and self-regulation.

I write books to help children understand their emotions and learn to control them.

I sincerely hope that your child enjoyed this story.

Would you mind taking a minute to leave your feedback?
Your opinion can help other parents choose this book.
I will be eternally grateful to you.

I am always happy to receive an e-mail from you.
To do this, write to the following e-mail address:
aleksharrisonwriter@gmail.com

Aleks

Printed in Great Britain
by Amazon